WILD
JOY
RIDES

Sophie Edina

© *2024 Sophie Edina*

ISBN Softcover: 978-3-384-35175-3

Cover & Chapter Artwork Design:
Sophie Edina via Canva Pro

Druck & Distribution
im Auftrag der Autorin:

tredition GmbH
An der Strusbek 10
22926 Ahrensburg
Germany

tredition GmbH
Abteilung "Impressumservice"
An der Strusbek 10
22926 Ahrensburg
Deutschland.

to those raised
on hope and ashes

Contents

Prologue

Yes, all of this is
t r u e ,
but not all of it was
real:

It's not about
t h e   b i r t h   o f   w o r d s
but how they make you
f e e l .

I. Introducing the Main Character

'what came first – the pain or the poetry?'

Autumn Blonde

It's August
but the love
in my chest
has *autumn leaves*
already.

Dying gracefully
like golden ashes
crumbling in my hands
after another summer
in the shade.

Silver Peony

(TW: war, hunger, loss)

I n s i d e   o f   m e
lives the soul
of my *grandmother*.

She was born on
N e w   Y e a r ' s   D a y
to a life
that would turn her fingers
stiff
from h o l d i n g   o n
to faith
and her heart achingly hollow
from all the times
f e a r
or e x h a u s t i o n
or g   r   i   e   f
would force their size
into her,
pushing innocence
out.

I was told
she had to *flee*
her home
leaving behind
childhood,
softness,

a *full* stomach
and the *laughter*
of her little brother.

Even if she now
r e s t s   b y   t h e   s e a
waves washing
over her soul
e n d l e s s l y
soothingly salty and fresh,
I am carrying
h e r   l e g a c y .

I still have dreams
in which I *run,*
waking to bones
aching to rest,
to be still
o   s o   s t i l l
on their own terms.

Echoes of her journey
keep rushing through me.
I wonder
how my own
will turn out.

Heirloom Lilac

I was a
poet fugitive.

A planet
in a distant orbit,

spat

      out

by a tribe
that couldn't
      keep   up
         with the speed
           of my moons.

Guided
by nothing
but
gravity,

finding her way
amongst
the
stars.

Pavement

(TW: terror, suicide, racism)

I was eight years old
when people
fell
from their offices

in their final and fatal
act of
f r e e d o m .

I was in sports class,
my father would tell me,
and the parents waited
to pick up their children
while watching
g r e y
consume Manhattan's skyline
on tube tv screens:

Sadistic symbolism
of the sudden absence
of *so many* things.

A day that feels like
a single moment
in which **noise** and s i l e n c e
collided
with a brutality
imagination would shy away from.

I grew up in a world
c o m a t o s e
then limping
then scared,

an ocean away
yet affected
by the simple truth
that *seconds*
could create
h I s t o r I c a l   m i l e s t o n e s
of loss,

grasping
how *fragile* normality is
and how thin the veil
between today
and no tomorrow.

I was s o   s c a r e d
and each year
it got *scarier*,

as my mind
m a t u r e d and *adjusted*
and the terror
sunk
deeper
under my skin

with every time
I'd rewatch people
fall

from their offices
and
g r e y
consume the Manhattan skyline,
everytime a plane flew
a bit too low
above my house at night.

What began as the
personal sensation of a child
grew into
a complex yet universal
mosaic of millions of fates,
millions of versions of fear
and grief
i n v a d i n g
my consciousness.

M o u r n i n g
people we never met
and possible lives
that were *ripped away*
from us and others,
mourn the consequences
of a day on which
the sun rose
just as it did today
and it will
tomorrow.

disenchanted
by the way
humanity was capable of

turning against itself
in an act of terrorism
of *unforeseen dimension,*

but also by
how it gave birth
to hatred
and distrust
people suffer from
to this day.

My mind will probably
never be
m a t u r e   or *adjusted*
enough to fit
t h e   f u l l   t r a g e d y
of 9/11
into it,

and that itself is something
I can hardly comprehend.

Raspberry Rose

She's *so young* -
when autumn comes
she still plays around
in the leaves;

Who would believe
she has some
d e m o n s
on her heels
already?

Bittersweet

(TW: self harm)

Another *sunset*.
Another golden lit reminder
that I am wasting
too
much
t i m e .

A n o t h e r   d a y   p a s s e d .
Another silver dagger
I pull out of someone's chest
just to *stab* it
into mine.

Orange Rust

How many cups of *tea*
will I chuck
with a
f a k e   s m i l e

until I can finally admit
w h i s k e y
is so much more
satisfying?

Old Gold

All the things
I love
rush into me in fall.

C h a n g e   i s   n e a r ;
You can see it
in the leaves
on the trees,
the alchemy
of the season changing
turning them to
g o l d .

In the morning ...
I can see my breath
and it makes me feel
s o   a l i v e .

In the afternoon ...
I watch the sun set
and it makes my skin
g l o w –
I feel so ripe.

I can smell
t h e   c i n n a m o n
the world is *dusted* with

I can taste
t h e   f l e s h
of *fresh* apples
on my tongue.

All the things
I love
are rushing into me
again:
That's when I know
          fall
has begun ...

Nirvana

How *lucky* I was
to have
fiction
as a h i d e a w a y .

Imaginary friends
made me
feel *comfortable*
with myself,

when r e a l people
rarely
accomplished that.

They at best
felt like *grinders*
and I payed with
m y s a w d u s t
to be shaped
in their presence.

I became
so conscious
of my form
and *so blind*
to what it holds
when they only

l o o k e d
at me.

When with stories
t h e   d e p t h   o f   m y   s o u l
didn't feel
like *purgatory*
anymore,

but like
a n   o c e a n
reflecting a night sky
and sometimes even
like *the sky itself*.

Desert Flower

You have to set
your heart
o n   f i r e

in order to see through
t h e   d a r k n e s s
of these days.

Cloud Dancer

She was made of *paper*.

Her destiny could have been
to search for poets
to
c o m p o s e   a n t h e m s
on her skin.

But she had a tendency
of getting too close
to
p y r o m a n i a c s ,
that would set her *on fire*
and then leave her
b u r n i n g .

Storm Blue

She didn't fall for
the good guys.

She'd always choose
the dark and twisted ones,
the bitter tastes,
the nightshade flowers,
t h e   m a z e s
at midnight.

That was the only
type of person
that *made sense*
to her.

The only
kind of people
she could
b e l i e v e   i n .

The only
kind of people
she could
b e l i e v e .

Moon Mist

I might attract
the sinners.
I might attract
t h e   s i n s .

They might be
moths
to my light bulb,
I might be
h o n e y
to them.

But maybe,
oh, maybe,
it's the other way
around.

And I only feel home
in a burned-out house
and I only find comfort
o n   t h e   g r o u n d .

Daybreak

The *Elderst Daughter* said:

‚Give me something
s o   b r o k e n
no one expects me
to fix it.

Give me something
s o   g r a n t
I will not have to
shrink myself
to fit into it.

Give me something
so painfully beautiful
It gives me permission
to run
from everything
I have ever known.'

And so the universe send
A man
like a *smoke cloud*
s h a r p   a n d   s h i n y
like a million
b r o k e n   m i r r o r s .

And it was the most
delicious sight
She'd ever seen.

II. Introducing the Cursed Nomad

'a trip through fall and back'

Amber Glow

Oh,
I remember.
Yes, I do.

I remember the chill
of the last August days –
how I close my eyes
to leap
i n t o a m b e r l I g h t .
into
          the
                    fall.

Oh,
I remember
how
          I
                    fall.

Woodsmoke

This autumn
smells an *aweful* lot
l i k e   g a s o l i n e
and I'm not sure yet
what that could mean.

Are we
s e t t i n g   f i r e
to the bridges
in our backs
or are we filling up
the tanks
to get away?

'It's fight or flight'
is what September
seems to say.
'Do what you have to do,
but you cannot stay.'

Black Iris

It was me,
you took by the hand
in a 4 a.m. storm,
and asked
h o w   f r e e
I intended to be,
for the rest
of this *one, insane life*.

Maple Sugar

You are
c o l d   n i g h t s
with *little clouds*
coming from our mouths
when we're talking
in a parking lot;

you are
o v e r s i z e d
sweaters and flannel shirts
that give me warmth
from the o u t s i d e
and from *within*;

you are
the smell of *camp fires*
and muddy shoes
and g a s o l i n e ;

you are
the *burning* taste of liquor
and my rebellious smile following,
my heart and my laugh light
because things feel *less frightening*
and more exciting
now.

You are
the wind that increases
every October
and that's blowing me towards
m y   o w n   r e c k l e s s n e s s ,

when the leaves slowly turn
into the colour of your eyes and
the sun sets so early
that I crave a place to *hide* in.

Golden Oak

Each Friday night
you *pour*
another glass of hope
for me –

another
a m b e r   p r o m i s e ,
that I swallow
right away.

Apple Cinnamon

Who needs
crowded streets
and
f o r e i g n   c i t y   m a z e s ,

when I can get lost
right here:

in the *wilds*
of your hair
on the backseat

in the d e p t h
of your moans
at the lookout

and

between the
c o n s t e l l a t i o n s
of the freckles
over your collarbone?

Hunter Green

H o m e
is wherever I feel
like *you love me*.

Celestial

It's 4 a.m. in the morning,
t h a t   a b s t r a c t   s p a c e
where not even
the shadows
move.

Waking from a dream
I recall
your *velvet* voice,

three words
at 4 a.m.
five months in.

You said you loved me,
and now I lie here
a n d   w o n d e r
if anything ever feels *real*
at 4 a.m. in the morning.

I wonder if it ever felt
r e a l
to you.

Bitter Chocolate

Don't feel sorry
It's okay,
go ahead,
don't worry,
I'm fine.

Thats the world
as we know it:
you will never be mine.
Alright.

Thats the life as I knew it
and I'm sick of the fight.

Just go.
Just go.
Just leave me now.

The things *truly*
turn out to be
the way
that they seem.

That's why it's *easier*
to dream.

Grey Dawn

It was me
the one who called you
a t   4   a . m .
on a Friday night,

just two weeks
after you said that
there was no use
in ending *good things*
in a fight.

So, you left
i n   s i l e n c e
as cruel
as words could never be.

And I guess this is
how free
you and me
are meant to be.

Peach Nectar

In your absence
my tongue *curls around*
t h e   f o r e i g n   e x p r e s s i o n s
your lips taught me.

French Roast

Another day of
s k i p p i n g   s o n g s
on my playlist,

but no line sticks
with me
like *the last words*
you said.

Another night
of denying
that in my dreams
I can still
feel
your kiss
on my lips
and your shirt
in my hand.

I t ' s   b e e n   a   y e a r
and
a part of me
knows
that this should be about
m y s e l f
and not about you.

That the *true fight*
I'm having
is with myself
and no
s h i n i n g   k n i g h t
can save me
from that,

but *I fell*
for you
and now
that another summer's passed

I'm falling
again,
like the
g o l d e n   l e a v e s
'cause
whatever this thing is
we had
I once declared it
' h o m e '
so I keep coming back
to that.

Deep Mahogany

Is this *more*
than a
l e s s o n   i n   h i s t o r y ,
what we have
shared
for *so long*?

In this season
I get *attracted*
by mystery,
d a r k   a n d   a d d i c t i v e ,
figuring out
to *which year*
we belong.

Striking Purple

'I'm not yours anymore',
I said
back then -
and now we're
s e p a r a t e d
by nothing
but a restaurant table
again.

Could've been
my weakness
that brought me back here:

My actions
unable to
c a t c h   u p
with my words.
My heart
unable to
l e t   g o .

But then
You raise your head
in a smile
And once again
I   f a l l
for the wrinkles

in the corners
of your eyes.

Precious fragments of seconds
before for the first time
I realize:

No need to run
anymore
from the man
I *adored*
when he's
r i g h t   h e r e   n o w
to *admire me*.

No need to
a t t a c h   s t r i n g s
to a soul *so free*,
when I'm free myself now,
strong myself now,
m y s e l f   now,
m y   o w n   now,
just how I once *lied* to be.

F i n a l l y
not just connected
in our tendency to
fall,
but in our ability to
get up again.

I'm not *yours* anymore,
I might have never been,
I'm *my own* now,

that's why
I ' m   b a c k
again.

Scarlet Sage

Maybe
we were meant
to meet again
just when
t h e   c r a c k s
in his heart
finally
matched mine.

Flame Scarlet

I guess
here we are again,
c r i m s o n   r e d   as ever.

Our minds *foggy*,
our fingers stiff,
l o n g   d r i v e s
and cold nights,
golden light
and your star sign rising.

Lavender Frost

'I'm not yours anymore
I'm my own now',

I said last summer,
then took
        t h e   f a l l
back into you.

Said *I'd be fine*
not keeping
the strings attached
but it turns out
they were
h o l d i n g   m e
together.

So now
I'm lying
on your pillow,
undressed
and *untangled*,
f r o z e n
in a state
between *us*
and tomorrow.

Gunmetal

(TW: death)

I wish
it was 4 a. m.

so *nothing* would
f e e l   r e a l

instead of
i n e v i t a b l y   d a r k
as right now at 2.

My heart is a
caged animal

my mind is
o n   t h e   l o o s e .

And I hurt
in silence,

d e a t h
e c h o i n g
i n   m y   b o n e s .

Copper

(TW: grief)

So this morning
I'm shedding
m y   s k i n .

I need the pastel
A u r o r a
paints the edges
of my world in

just before
t h e   s u n   i s   r i s i n g
to find a place
to begin again.

And here I am:
collecting whats now
s c a t t e r e d
like scared chicken
and shattered
like cursed mirror sheds.

M e m o r i e s
to guide me,
weave my own story from,
now that someone
cut our threads.

In the wake
of the *wake*
of a life by your side,
waiting for
t h e   g o l d e n   l i g h t
to *kiss* the bruises
of a lost fight
goodnight.

And I will *mourn* you
till your bones are save
and overrun
w i t h   w i l d f l o w e r s   a n d   i v y .

You just don't get away
with *getting away* like that
after all those years
beside me.

Happy times
l i k e   b u t t e r f l i e s
will *rest* on me
whenever I stay
still enough,
and *Auroras glowing kiss*
will remind
my bitter lips
whenever She
defeats the dark
o f   t h e   c r u e l   a b s e n c e
of your love.

Forest Night

'Cause who once
tasted raindrops
e y e t o e y e
with the wild
will never again
be afraid
of the night.

They will wander
in darkness,
no need for a light,
but in need of
a soul
w a n d e r i n g , t o o .

Oh, all the miles
that I wandered
with you ...

Maroon

(TW: grief)

It's been a year
since you've been *gone*
and I still
haven't written to you
since.

Braiding
silent goodbyes
into barbed wire fences,
letting
lost heartbeats
tumble away
in the wind.

And I'm fine with that
most days.

But today,
oh today,
I wish it was still just
a flaky picket fence
and *golden light*
between us …

I hope
it's still fall
where you are.

III. Introducing the Charming Rouge
(TW: toxic relationship)

'finding yourself in someone else's darkness'

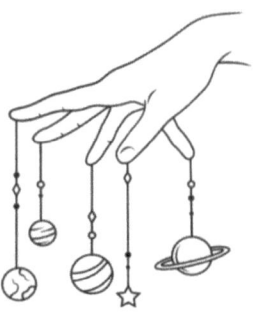

Orchid Tint

I was
w a s h e d   a s h o r e
at a place
so peaceful,
welcoming me
with the
m o s t   o p e n   a r m s .

'But what if this detour
Becomes a whole new journey?',
my voice
still shaking
from solitude
asked.

Not ready
to *rest,*
Not ready
to s e t t l e ,
so scared
of the *urgency*
with which my heart
b e g g e d
to heal.

Still ready
to *fight,*

so eager
to h i d e ,
so scared
and yet
s o   d e t e r m i n e d
to feel.

Arrowwood

Oh it calls
my name,
how can I be sure
that I'm not meant to
give in?

If it knows me so well,
Maybe
I b e l o n g   there,
maybe
it's where I come from.

Falcon

Look at me
I'm just a sack of
l o o s e   b o n e s
at your doorstep.

Please
make a person
out of me,
or at least
make it
m a k e   s e n s e .

Frozen Dew

I was a loner:
the *tightest knot*
in a
house of twisted souls.

And, oh,
then you came,
a n   e n i g m a
of your own,
unbothered
by my walls.

When I moved in
I said to *him*
I was sure
I couldn't stay.

But magnetically *charged*
by your finger tips,
I also
couldn't stay away.

Deep Well

There was
t h i s   b e a s t
inside of me
I *pretended*
I didn't understand,

hoping it would
morph itself
into a bad dream.

But it was my soul
roaring
from the cage
I shoved it in.

It was my heart
playing only by
its *own* rules.

It was my truth
p i e r c i n g the dark
like a laser beam.

So *forceful*
it could hurt,
so *sharp*
it could come of harsh,

but so *bright*
I couldn't look away
from myself.

Gothic Grape

Picture loneliness
so *deep*
it becomes
l o n g i n g .

Picture a shadow
born *in a pit*
craving touch
s o   u r g e n t l y
it begs to be scared.

Picture a soul
bruised
by its own softness
over and over,
and then
finding
that there are shades
darker than purple.

Picture me
leaving
t h e   g r a v e   o f   m y   y o u t h
to encounter a house
full of beasts.

Of course
I felt like I
belonged.

Of course
staring down
t h e   p r e c i p i c e
o f   y o u r   e y e s
wasn't a threat
but an *invitation*.

Peach Blossom

I was *raised*
to be scared
of addiction –

laced myself
into a corset
of restraint
to never breath in
t o o   m u c h   p l e a s u r e
at once.

So when I met you
I was gasping for air
so hungrily
that i had you
u n d r e s s   m e
your fingers
t e a r
all my caution away
before my guard
could catch up

Good thing,
you can't get addicted
to people ...

Or so I thought.

Roan Rouge

All my life
I felt so *paper thin*
couldn't stop
the rain
the pain
e a c h   s h a m e f u l   s t a i n
from settling
under my skin.

Couldn't be my own
when I only *lived*
to be
w r i t t e n   o n .

Couldn't grow
when I never *escaped*
s u r v i v a l   m o d e .

Couldn't let my powers *bloom*
in a garden
that was vandalised
b y   w e e d s   o f   d o u b t .

Couldn't let my wisdom *shine*
in a home
that was designed
to keep the *light out*.

And then
I met you,

b o l d
as a lightning,
c l o s e d
like a circuit,
a forcefield
in which
I could finally sense
m y o w n f o r m , too.

No *touches*,
j u s t s p a r k s .
No *walls up*,
j u s t h e a r t s –

meeting
and beating
in the way
they were born to.

Flame Scarlet

I never hoped
to come out of this
unscarred,

there's a price
you have to pay
when you're ready
to have all your
inner roadmaps
t o r n   a p a r t .

I didn't even ask
for poetry
in return.

In fact
I hoped for
a l l   o f   m y   p a g e s
to burn.

Hydrangea

I'm growing
l i k e   a   b l u e   f l a m e
these days

since you let me
　　　　dive
　　　　　　　into the depth
　　　　　　　　　　of your soul.

I'm charged
with the certainty
that I could
h o l d   i t   a l l .

Spreading myself
o v e r   t h e   p l a n e s
o f   p o t e n t i a l –
silent splits
and the heat
so deliciously dangerous
only for myself
and for you
to see.

True power
comes
quietly

just like
t r u e a d m i r a t i o n
does.

So *come*
and lay your hands
on me
dare to be *burned*
by what you
u n r a v e l e d .

Mood Indigo

So
they warned me
about your
d e p t h ,

as if I hadn't
been standing
o n   t h e   c l i f f s i d e
contemplating to *jump*
anyway.

They feared
I'd be *tempted*
by false promises,

when I had only learned
i n   t h e   c r u e l e s t   w a y
that *nothing*
can ever
be certain.

They believed
your darkness
could harm
m y   l i g h t ,
when I had always been
a creature of the night.

Solar Power

He was *so bright*
in all the right ways:
The closer I got to him
the larger
m y   s h a d o w   g r e w .

But that's *all right,*
so did my wings
so did
a l l   o f   m e .

I had no idea
about the height
o f   m y   p o t e n t i a l ,
about the size
o f   m y   t r u e   f o r m .

Risking *blindness*
in the meantime
seemed like a price
worth paying.

Charisma

The rush of
s u r v i v i n g   h i m
was *too strong*

to stay away
for long.

Purple Opulence

You had this thing
where the *tight grip*
of your hands
never felt like
a n   a c t   o f   v i o l e n c e
to me.

You had the ability
to convey
all those things
people would
g i v e   h u g s
for,

c o m f o r t ,
r e s p e c t ,
r e a s s u r a n c e ,
l o v e ,
every time
our skin
connected.

Spicy Orange

Having you
inside of me
felt like
f r e s h   b l o o d
in my mouth:

A pain
so *primal,*
a rush
so *intimate,*

predator and prey
delicately braided
into the *fuse*
of
m y   e x t a s y .

Astral Aura

You said
I was *more*
than
t h e   m o o n
to you
– even more than
t h e   s u n .

Touching me
vowing
you in fact
thought of me
as a
        s o l a r
                s y s t e m ,

all I could reply
was that
technically

that made you

a
black
hole.

Billowing Sail

But I was
a good girl
after all.

I realized some souls
were
w a y t o o d e e p
to jump
and then survive

       the
             fall.

I h i t t h e b r e a k s
before someone could
pull the trigger.

T o o k a s t e p b a c k
from the abyss
because
my urge to live
grew bigger.

I couldn't stay.
I promised
to him
and *myself*

and to you,

and so
I sneaked out
a t   t h e   b r e a k   o f   d a w n
like us
creatures of the night
tend to do.

Shifting Sand

I still remember
how your hands
t a u g h t m e

that there were forms
o f p o e t r y
that weren't soft
at all.

IV. Introducing the Soft Mage

'too sweet to last long'

Liberty

I ran into you
i n   s i l e n c e .

The silhouette of a cowboy
in front of worshipped canvas,
sharp edges and **bold strokes**,
but
a   s t i l l   l i f e
nonetheless.

We were
wonderers and   w a n d e r e r s
in need to add a *sense* to us.

Our story was just
a n   e m p t y   b o t t l e ,
that could ride
the currents
across the sea

but   b r e a k   and *cut* you
like a heart
so devastatingly easily.

Vintage Indigo

I write him hymns,
as soon as sunshine regains
its *golden quality*,
but sometimes,
b e t w e e n   l i n e s ,
a certain *loneliness* emerges.

And I recall
s t o p p i n g   y o u
on our way to a gallery,
head full of *loose threads*
of conversations
we b r a i d e d through our days.

I recall the *urgency*
in which my heart
was *beating*
within a second,
unexpected,
a   b o l d   b e a t
to a melody
that
s t o p p e d   m e
in our *casual* ways.

I needed to know
right then,

how my own
r e c k l e s s n e s s
would *taste*
if it collided
with your
charms.

How the tunes
my heart produced
would *alter*
if they were placed
next to yours,
within your arms.

O   D a r l i n g ,
October weekends have nothing
on our months in Brooklyn,
stirring my coffee
your smile is still with me,
back in this
illuminated cafe
in New York City.

Macadamia

When I said,
we were
t h e   s a m e

I meant
you were *half fiction*
and *half magic*
while I was
f u l l   p o e t r y .

Not *interchangeable*
exactly
but terribly hard
to tell apart.

Potters Clay

There's this
funny thing
I wanted to tell you about:

Lately
it's you
that I feel
in my poetry.

Tiger's Eye

Knee deep
in this daydream
already,
b e n d i n g   l i g h t
to see you grin,

can't wait for
a *real* real life
t o   r u n   f r o m
and having *you*
to hide in.

Botanical Garden

I gifted you
m y s i l e n c e
- *a reckless leap of faith to me* –

and in return
you lit
f i r e w o r k s
on my lips

and turned
the moths
in my chest,
one by one,
into soaring
b u t t e r f l i e s ...

Almost Mauve

Coming from
d e p r e s s i o n
and *anxiety*

you are the best reason
for wasting
t h e   c o l d   a n d   d a r k   d a y s
in the comfort of this bed

I had in years.

Forget-Me-Not

(TW: suicide)

I let you have it
that place of your own
buried
in your mind.

If you *demanded*
to be lonely,
I'd be the last one
to deny it.

After all
all that we know
is what *reflects*
within ourselves.

I always sensed
darkness
in you,
heaviness
on the lower shelves.

Yet all that was in reach
for most:
your kindness,
your fragility.

So maybe
I was *tricked* to think
I did heal you like
y o u   h e a l e d   m e .

T h e   m i n o r   c r a c k s
around my heart
so *easy* for your hands
to mend,

seems like
there's just
ink
left to ask now
why
l o n e l i n e s s
got you
in the end.

Star Sapphire

Funny thing is
I still do remember
Winter in Williamsburg;
lingering September;

sunshine,
O, s u n s h i n e
brick walls & blue tea,
the delicate serenade
of you looking back
at me ...

V. Introducing Reality

'that's the thing with fiction – it only
ever lasts a moment.
But so does reality.'

Ginger Snap

With every drop
of energy
life *squeezes*
o u t   o f   m e

it *pushes* me
closer to
one of two options:

One is
g i v i n g   u p
but the other one is
f i n d i n g   p e a c e .

Cloudbourst

(TW: anxiety, depression)

Fear wasn't
a pair of glasses
anymore
that slightly altered view.

It had grown into
a f u l l e x o s k e l e t o n .

It might have
protected me,
but it made me feel

so heavy,
        so isolated,
                so foreign.

It became
its own reason
to hold back.

It became its
own source
o f s a d n e s s .

A self-fulfilling prophecy
that it could only hurt
t o b e f r e e .

What price
did I pay
to stay *save*?

It made me
the crumbling statue
of the hero
I then had to *invent*
to be saved by.

Obsidian

The thing
we have to learn
o n o u r o w n
is that
we cannot *choose*
the people
we gravitate towards.

But
we *choose*
h o w   f a r we wade
into their wilderness.
we choose
the gear
we take with us.
We chose
when we rest
or turn around.

We might not choose
who we love
but we choose
how we allow them
to love us.

Oxford Tan

Raised on *fairy tales*,
I was left to wonder
if the villain in this story
was going to be
myself or
the rest of the world –

but all those detours in fall
taught me:
I'd either fight
for my p e r s o n a l   p e a c e
and risk to be
the *villain*
in someone else's story

or bow to any
invading force
and chain my soul
to their throne.

Dusky Orchid

(TW: toxic relationships)

The villains
all are *female* here
but the heroes are, too.

Got my heart b r o k e n
by *make belief*
and then by you.

I said
it's *tough love*
and they said
i t ' s   t o x i c
I said
I *knew* that
but I could take it.

All those people
b r u i s i n g   m y   r i b c a g e
in exchange for a hug.

I can love
about *anybody*
but F U C K -
I think it's time
to finally
love myself.

Reflecting Pond

There is no denying:

We all crave
t r a g e d y
it's so *sharp* and *condensed,*
o so poisonous
and o so potent,
a p o t i o n o f p o t e n t i a l –
every artists fuel.

But
that doesn't mean
we have to carry it
inside ourselves.

There is
enough sadness
in the world already
enough s a d n e s s
enough t r a u m a
enough b r o k e n h e a r t s
reflecting the light.

We don't need
to become
another well of the same old
human darkness

there is enough to share,
to lend,
t o   r e l e a s e
from its cells .

And from now on
I might.

Pastel Lilac

This September
things are *different,*

because
t h e   s k y   i s   l i l a c
and not gold.

because
I   d o n ' t   h a v e   t o   r u n
anywhere
to get home.

because
my youth
s t i l l   l i v e s   i n   m e
and I've become
its *guardian.*

because I turned the clocks
backwards
            and still   m o v e d   o n .

because
it's my own shoes
I walk in now
when I need to
f e e l   s t r o n g .

Pear Sorbet

Just imagine:
A poem
written by me.

About how
I started the morning
by listening
to the *birds cooing*
a n d   t h e   w i n d
in the trees.

And how
I walked my dog
through *sand*
and *fallen leaves*
smelling a u t u m n
and t h e   s e a
at once.

How
I got myself
a cup of coffee
after breakfast
and *layed in bed*
for a while.

Took a shower
to get ready
to be
M E –

the writer
in a coastal town,
painted white
since the royals came here
for their holidays.

Being
a little *lonely*,
a little e m p t y ,
and quiet enough
to become
a m a g n e t
to the *poetry*
and the *art*
the universe has
s c a t t e r e d a r o u n d
this place.

Winter Sky

I couldn't even tell you
how old I was
when we first met.

I was too old:
Too old to have
an imaginary friend,
old enough to know
how r e b e l l   s t o r y l i n e s
end.

Yet I was too young:
Too young to drown
in muddy green eyes,
but *young enough* to run
and m a k e   i t   o u t alive.

And look at me now:
E s c a p e d   my twenties,
had one *hell of a ride*.

I might have been
too young
for quite a lot of things
but now I'm old enough
to know
which ones I got right.

Blushing Bride

(TW: loss)

You know
what it means,
don't you?

A feeling of
f i v e   l e t t e r s :
The pain of
letting go
over and over
again.

A n   o c e a n   o f   m e m o r i e s
and two *hollow* hands
pushing through them
towards *something*
that's not
a fight for survival
anymore.

Because
you don't just
grief *people*,
not just   l o s e   t h e m
to a grave.

You also have to burry
choices

you couldn't m a k e
chances
you couldn't t a k e
feelings
you could t a s t e
but never *swallow*
until it was
too late.

Red Plum

Love,
      love,
            love.

It is nothing
to *learn*
But to f i n d .

And Time might

tear
      it
           down,

like it does
to all g r e a t m o n u m e n t s
of humankind,

The sensation might
f a d e
but the knowledge
h o w g r a n t
h o w g o l d e n
h o w r e a l
it is

will *never*
        leave you
                again.

Stillwater

Pale blue
m e m o r i e s ,
vows
of juvenile admiration.

We were *so young*,
matching cuts
h e a l e d b a c k
to matching scars –

Imagine where we'd be
without *nurturing*
our imagination.

Bossa Nova

Do you *remember*
our very first
F i f t h   o f   S e p t e m b e r ?

'Cause I recall
sitting in a fast food place,
had three *handmade* songs
to sing to you.

We might have really been
pretenders
then,
but wise we got with time,
w e   g r e w .

Was it really
that pretentious, though?
Despite our youth,
w e   k n e w
what we could do.

And you can't *fake poetry*.
If you do
it's just *some lines* that rhyme.

You cant *fake love*
and *hope*

and *loyalty*!

I must have sensed it
at the time:

I'd watch you g r o w
and lend you a hand
if you needed it.

For what I know
It's our *foes*
that got defeated.

Y o u   s t a y e d   a f l o a t,
holding on
to *imagination*
while demons drowned
in doubts
and disorientation.

Chasing horizons
to find a place
to plant
y o u r   p o t e n t i a l;
now fruit and herbs
and flowers *blossom*.

Life's *not* a battle
if you embrace
t h e   a d v e n t u r e .

Looking back
all those years
I gifted you my words
t h e y   g r e w
from harvesting
your seeds.

Happy birthday,
my dear,
muse
and hero
and friend,
may next year
s h o w e r   y o u
in treats.

Juniper

You can't
pull yourself
out of the gutter
h o l d i n g o n
to just
your own very soul.

But you can
r e a c h o u t
to someone else's hand.

So how about
we hold on to
each other,

so we can
g e t o u t
together?

I want to watch
you
make this world
y o u r o w n .

Tangerine

Go ahead
and search the lines
t h a t   I   w r i t e
for a proof,

when the truth's
just as *thin*
as the paper
(I use):

You see
t h e   l i g h t
shining through.

The *golden glow*
of your soul
turns every place
into
h o m e ,

Calypso Coral

Capturing
love in poetry
Is like

capturing
t h e   s p a r k s
our hearts produce
when *colliding*.

And in the *heat*
and the *light* of it
we set ourselves on fire
to burn
f o r   a n y t h i n g
our souls long for.

Change
and *compassion*
and
p h o e n i x e s   r i s i n g
from the ashes …

Burgundy

I'd rather sip on red wine
and rest *against you*
by the campfire

than let my mouth
turn *sour*
over other peoples'
frowns and murmur.

O,
constellations and spells
and *nothing else.*

Let's just be
a magical mess
together
with my head
on your shoulder,
facing the stars;

lips *cold*
and
hands *warm.*

Hibiscus

Souls
       so
              deep

to survive in the dark
t h e y j u s t s h i n e ,

we're *messy,*
we're *messed up,*
but w e ' r e f i n e ,

We live in the flickers,
oh, we *glow*
and we g r o w ,

Souls
       so
              deep

you can't help

but
       fall
              for us,
                     oh.

Epilogue

I made
s o m e t h i n g
It's right here
in my palm:

Still *fresh*
and *warm*.

I made it myself,
made it pretty,
prettier,
e v e n   p r e t t i e r ,
so you would look at
i t
instead of *me*.

This is what
I want you
to *see*;

t h e   b e a u t y
I harvest
from my mind;
the *sum*
of your taste
and my hands

c o m b i n e d .

Something *soft*
and *round*
as easy to hold
as to
s w a l l o w   w h o l e .

Would you smile
at it?
D o u b l e   t a p ?
would you let it
touch
your soul?

About the Author

Sophie Edina

is a passionate introvert (*INFJ*), fiction and poetry writer and psychologist. She is an advocate for mindful representation of mental health issues and queerness.

Sophie lives in Germany with her partner and their dog, dreaming of the Scottish sky while forgetting about another cup of tea she just made.

She previously published *'Wild Fire Flies'* and *'Wild Heart Beats'* as the first two installments of the *'Wild World Words'* poetry series.

Follow @*sophie_edina* on Instagram or visit www.sophie-edina.com for updates!

Zeitfracht Medien GmbH
Ferdinand-Jühlke-Straße 7
99095 Erfurt, Deutschland
produktsicherheit@kolibri360.de